For Mum, Dad, Kevin, Lisa and Pauline

With love – M.E.

EGMONT
We bring stories to life

First published 2011
by Egmont UK Limited
239 Kensington High Street, London W8 6SA

ISBN HB 978 1 4052 5358 1
ISBN PB 978 1 4052 5359 8

A CIP catalogue record for this title is available
from The British Library

1 3 5 7 9 10 8 6 4 2

Printed in China

Poggle
and the Birthday Present

M I C H A E L   E V A N S

EGMONT

Poggle was pumping air into a new beach ball.

"Nearly done," he said.

Henry looked worried.
"I think you should . . ."

"...stop."

"Whoops,"
said Poggle,
"too much air."

The beach ball was
a birthday present
for their friend, Lily.

"It's Lily's birthday today," said Henry,
"and now we haven't got a present."

Poggle scratched his head.

"Let's look for a new one
on the beach," he said.

"Good idea," said Henry.
"We might find a genie in a bottle,
or a treasure chest,
or a magic carpet, or . . ."

They walked to the beach
with Henry talking
all the way.

But they didn't find any of Henry's things.
What they did find was a . . .

knobbly stick,

some seaweed,

an old hat,

a worm,

a thingymebob

and an
empty shell that turned out
not to be empty.

"These are no good,"
said Poggle.

"I like the seaweed," said Henry
putting it on his head.
"**Roar!** I'm a sea monster!"

Poggle laughed and
Henry chased him.

Henry bumped into Poggle who
had suddenly stopped running.

"Look," said Poggle. "A giant shell."

"That's huge," said Henry
rubbing his nose.

The shell was slightly open, so Henry looked inside.

"Hello!" he shouted.

"Hello!" replied a voice.

"There's someone in there," Henry whispered.

"It's only an echo," said Poggle. "Listen."

"Iggle piggle wiggle tickle," he shouted.

"Iggle piggle wiggle tickle," echoed Poggle's voice.

Henry and Poggle shouted
funny names into the shell.

"Hoot boot lumpy pickle!"

"Wizzle wazzle woo hoo!"

"I'm going to explore inside," said Henry when
they had finished shouting.

With an effort he climbed into the shell.
His feet had just disappeared
when . . .

Snap!

. . . the shell shut.

"Hey!"
cried Henry.
"Let me out."

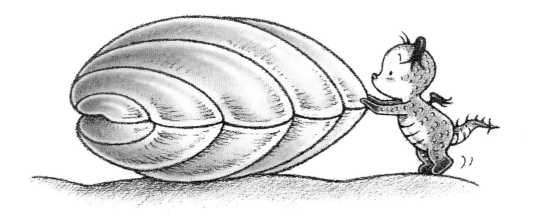

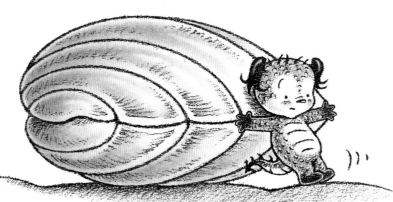

Poggle tried everything
to open the shell but it
wouldn't budge.

How was he going to
get Henry out?

"It's smelly in here," said a muffled Henry.
"I need some fresh air."

That's it, thought Poggle.
"I'll be back in a while," he shouted.
And he ran off.

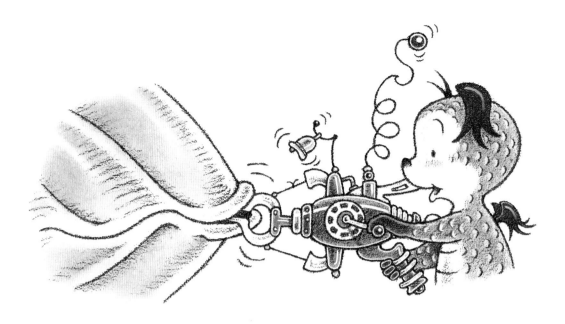

Poggle returned carrying the thingymebob and a pump.
He wiggled the thingymebob into the shell.

Then he turned its handle.

Twang! Whirl! Ping!

The thingymebob had made a small opening.
It was just big enough to put
the pump into.

Poggle pumped air into the shell until . . .
there was a creak
and a crack
and a . . .

The shell burst open.

Henry flew through the air like a superhero.
He landed with a puff in the soft sand.

Poggle ran to Henry.
"Are you all right?" he asked.

Henry grinned.
"That was fun," he said. "Let's do it again."

But Poggle wasn't listening.

He bent down
  and picked something up.

"Look what else came out of the shell," he said.
And he held out a gigantic pearl.

Henry gasped.

"We've found Lily's birthday present!"
said Poggle.

"It's the best
birthday present
EVER,"
said Henry.

And it was.